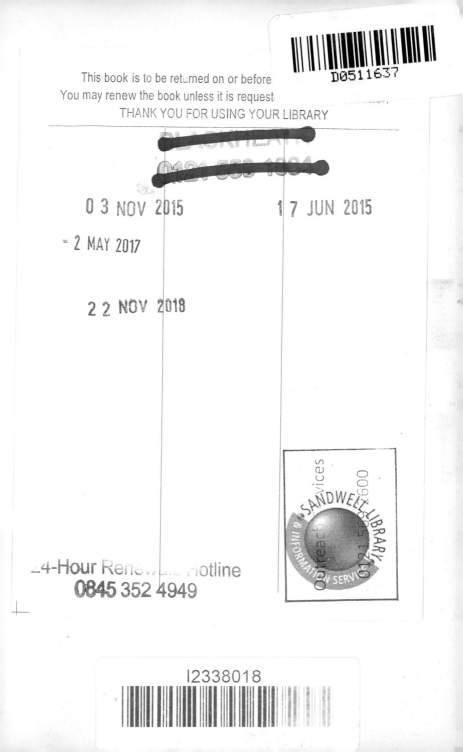

First published in 2010 in Great Britain by
Barrington Stoke Ltd
18 Walker St, Edinburgh, EH3 7LP

www.barringtonstoke.co.uk

ISBN: 978-1-84299-821-2

Printed in Great Britain by Bell & Bain Ltd

Contents

Chapter 1
The Magic Cauldron

In the middle of Wales there was a lake.

A cold, grey lake.

In the middle of the lake there was a castle.

In the castle lived the witch, Ceridwen.

Ceridwen was so powerful that the grass bowed before her and the waves drew back from her feet. She lived with her husband and a son called Morfran, which means Sea Crow in Welsh.

One day she looked at her son and saw how very ugly he was.

"Look at you!" she snapped. "You're all hunched up and your nose looks like a beak! What girl is going to want to marry you?"

Morfran wiped his nose. "Then do something about it, Mother," he said. "You're a witch, make me look good."

Ceridwen went to her study and took out her spell books. The books had dragon skin covers and the spells were written in silver ink. Eyes peeped from between the lines. Bats flitted in their pages.

She looked for a spell to make her son handsome but none of them would work. They were too weak. Then, at the back of the book, in secret writing, she found the weirdest spell of all. It would not make Morfran good-looking but it might help him find a wife.

"I'll use this spell," Ceridwen said. "Morfran will be able to sing wonderful songs. He'll be the best bard in Wales. He'll know all the magic spells. He'll be the best sorcerer and wizard. And he'll be able to turn himself into anything he wants – he'll be a shape-shifter."

She went on, "This spell will make Morfran the greatest bard and sorcerer and shape-shifter in the whole world. *Then* someone will want to marry him."

So Ceridwen set to work.

She took her great, bronze cooking pot, her witch's cauldron.

She filled it with cold lake water.

She dropped in magic herbs, secret words, starlight.

She set a fire to burn under it.

The cauldron grew warm, then hot. The potion began to brew and boil. Ceridwen stood back and rubbed her hands and folded her arms. "Now," she said, "someone must stir this spell. They must stir and never stop, for a year and a day. Who's going to do that?"

"Not me," said her husband.

"Not me," said Morfran her son.

So she found the smallest servant in the castle and dragged him down to the kitchen. "You'll have to do it," she said, "and never, ever stop stirring!"

The servant was a boy called Gwion.

He took a big wooden spoon and began to stir.

He stirred for days and nights.

He stirred for weeks and months.

He stirred sitting and lying down and kneeling.

He stirred awake and asleep.

He stirred twelve spoons to splinters.

At last, the year and the day came to an end.

Ceridwen came and sat down by the cauldron, watching with her sharp eyes. She knew that when the spell was ready the potion would bubble, and three hot drops of magic would splash out. All the power of the spell would be in those drops. She was ready to catch them for her son.

But as she watched Gwion stir and stir she felt tired.

Her head nodded.

She fell asleep.

Gwion gave one last great splosh. Suddenly the potion bubbled. Before he could jump away, three drops splashed out onto his hand. They were so hot they burned him. "Ouch," he said. He put his hand to his mouth and he licked up the drops.

As soon as he did that he felt the magic go through him like a flash of lightning.

Like a great cry.

Like a stab of pain.

He saw the future.

He saw the past.

He saw all the secrets of the world.

He was a bard and a sorceror and a shape-shifter.

And he knew that when Ceridwen woke up she would be mad with anger, because he had stolen the magic that she'd made for her son.

He dropped the spoon. He climbed out of the window. He rowed across the lake.

And he ran.

Chapter 2
The Shape-shifter

The first thing Ceridwen saw when she woke up was the spoon lying on the floor. She opened her eyes wide and gave a screech of anger.

Gwion was gone. The fire was out. The cauldron had stopped boiling.

Ceridwen knew what had happened. As she stared, the cauldron cracked and fell apart, and the rest of the useless spell flowed out across the floor and into the lake.

Ceridwen jumped up and ran outside. She leapt across the lake in one huge step and raced off after the thief.

Gwion was running. He ran over hills and valleys. But he saw her coming behind him, like the shadow of a cloud, and he couldn't run fast enough. She was catching up with him.

He thought, *I'm a shape-shifter now. I must do something!*

He turned himself into a hare and sped away.

Ceridwen yelled, "You won't get away like that!"

She turned herself into a greyhound and sped after him.

They raced up hills and through forests. Soon Ceridwen's teeth were snapping at his heels, but just at that moment Gwion came to a fast flowing river.

Gwion threw himself in. He became a salmon, swimming fast and strong.

Ceridwen yelled, "You won't get away like that!"

She turned herself into an otter and dived in after him.

They swam through weeds and waves. Soon Ceridwen's teeth were snapping at his tail, but at that moment he came to a waterfall.

Gwion leapt into the air. He became a swallow, flying swift and high.

Ceridwen yelled, "You won't get away like that!"

She turned herself into a hawk and soared after him.

They swooped through clouds and storms. Soon Ceridwen's beak was snapping at his feathers, and this time he knew he was in trouble. He was out of breath too.

What can I do now? he thought.

He looked down and saw that he was flying over a farm-yard. The farmer had been sifting the corn, and all over the farm-yard lay hundreds of tiny seeds of corn. That gave Gwion an idea. He dropped down and turned himself into a seed of corn and lay there, hidden among the hundreds of others.

She'll never find me here, he thought.

Ceridwen circled down and perched on the fence and looked at the farm-yard with her sharp eyes. She was still angry, and she wasn't going to give up now. She wanted to get her own back. She wanted her revenge.

"You won't get away like that either," she snapped. "You're not the only one who's clever, little thief Gwion!"

Ceridwen hopped down among the corn. She turned herself into a black hen.

And she pecked up every seed of corn in the farm-yard.

Every single one.

Then she went back to her castle in the lake and sat in her chair.

"Where's little Gwion?" Morfran asked.

"Dead," she said. "I've eaten him."

But that night, as the moon shone through the window, she felt a soft stirring inside her. And she wondered if he was really dead. Because after all, now he was a bard, and a sorceror, and a shape-shifter.

Every month, as the moon grew and shrank, Ceridwen knew that Gwion was still alive. He was growing inside her, a new baby. And she knew at the end of nine months, he would be born.

"You won't get away like that!" she snapped. "I'll deal with you once and for all."

But when the baby was born his face was so beautiful and so bright and shining she looked at him and found she wasn't sure about killing him any more. She felt annoyed at herself.

"Well, I'll still have my revenge," she said.

She took a small leather bag and she put the baby inside. Then she took him to the river, and she threw the bag onto the water and watched it bob away.

"Good-bye, thief Gwion," she said.

Then she went back to her castle in the lake and sat in her chair.

"Where's little Gwion?" Morfran asked.

"Dead," she said. "I've drowned him."

But that night, as the moon shone on the river, there was a soft stirring inside the leather bag. And the bag floated gently on the surface, past forests and villages, down to the sea.

The bag bobbed against a row of wooden poles called a weir, made to catch fish.

And there it stopped.

Chapter 3
The Shining Face

Now the king of that country was King Gwyddno, and his castle was nearby. Gwyddno had a son called Elffin. Everyone called him Prince Elffin the Unlucky, because nothing ever went right for him. Gwyddno said to his son, "It's about time you had some luck. Go down to the weir. Every year, on May Eve, there's at least a hundred pounds worth of salmon caught in that weir. This year you can have what you find there. Maybe it will change your life."

Elffin was pleased. He kissed his wife Anwen. "Good luck," she said. He took his horse and rode down to the weir. When he got there the sun was rising, and the river rippled into the sea.

But there was not a single fish in the weir.

Not even one.

Elffin looked up and down the river. The only thing he could see was a small leather bag bobbing against one of the wooden poles.

"You really are unlucky, Prince," one of the servants said. "This fish trap always has fish in it. But this year there's nothing but an old bag someone's thrown away.

Elffin got down from his horse. "Well, I may as well see what's in it. Maybe it's something worth a hundred pounds."

The servant laughed. "Why bother?"

But Elffin took off his boots and walked out into the stream. The water was cold and it rushed against him. When he got to the bag he grabbed it and held it high as he made his way back, soaked up to his waist.

He opened the bag.

There smiling up at him, was a baby boy, with the most lovely face he had ever seen, full of intelligence and beauty.

The servant stared. "What a bright face!"

"Then that's what we'll call him," Elffin said. "His name will be Taliesin." (Which means bright face in Welsh.)

He climbed back up on his horse and put the boy in front of him. He rode very carefully back to his father's castle. But he was gloomy because he knew his father would be angry that there were no fish.

He gave a great sigh.

At once, to his amazement, the baby spoke. "Don't be sad, Prince Elffin."

Elffin stared. "You can talk!"

"More than that," Taliesin said, "I'm a bard. And here's my first song."

So he sang –

"Don't cry, Prince Elffin.

Never in Gwyddno's weir

Has anyone found a treasure like me.

Though I'm tiny, I'm talented.

From deep in the river

I'll bring you good luck.

On the day you're in trouble

I'll be more use than salmon."

Elffin had never heard such a sweet and clever song.

"Are you human?" Elffin asked. "Or are you a spirit out of the river?"

Taliesin laughed. "What am I?" He began to sing again.

"I was a thief of magic.

Chased by an angry hag.

I fled as a hare.

I swam as a salmon.

I soared as a swallow.

Was a seed on the floor.

Nine months in darkness.

Sailed away in a bag.

I've been dead.

I've been alive.

Once I was Gwion.

Now I'm Taliesin."

Elffin couldn't wait to get home. He ran
into the castle, where his wife Anwen and his
father King Gwyddno were waiting.

"Well?" the King said, "have you brought
your catch?"

"This is my catch!" Elffin laid the baby
boy on the floor.

"What good is he?" Gwyddno groaned.

"I'm more use than a few fish," Taliesin
said softly.

Gwyddno stared. "He can talk! But he's just a baby!"

Elffin laughed. "He's Taliesin. And he's going to be our bard."

He picked up the baby and gave him to his wife. And Anwen smiled down at the shining face.

"More than that," she said. "He'll be just like our son."

Chapter 4
The Great Feast

Taliesin grew up to be wise and clever. By the time he was thirteen he could out-magic any sorceror and out-sing any bard. Elffin and Anwen loved him dearly, and Elffin grew more rich and no one called him Unlucky any more.

That year King Maelgwn of North Wales invited all the kings of Wales to a great Christmas feast. King Gwyddno was happy to go. He took a hundred servants with him, and he took his son Elffin too.

"But be careful," he said to Elffin. "Don't say anything stupid. Maelgwn is a very powerful king, and he has a terrible temper. He has the best of everything, and hates it if anyone thinks they're better than him."

Elffin said good-bye to his wife and to Taliesin. "I'll be back after Christmas," he said. "Everything will be fine."

He climbed on his horse.

Anwen looked worried. "I wish Taliesin was going with you."

Elffin laughed. "Don't worry! Nothing bad will happen."

Taliesin said nothing, but he climbed to the top of the castle and watched them ride away.

He was worried too.

****

At Maelgwn's palace the feast was more splendid than anyone had ever seen. Maelgwn and his queen sat on thrones in their great hall. Thousands of kings and knights and ladies and bards and bishops sat around them. The food was splendid. The clothes were splendid. The horses and dogs were splendid. The music was splendid.

Every hour one of Maelgwn's twenty-four bards got up and sang a new song to tell the King how splendid he was.

At first Elffin enjoyed it all. But as time went on he began to get annoyed.

Everyone was talking about one thing. "Who has a better wife than Maelgwn's?" they asked each other. "No one. Who has better horses than Maelgwn's? No one. Who has better bards than Maelgwn's?"

"*I have*," Elffin said.

Everyone stopped talking and stared at him.

"Be quiet!" his father whispered.

But Elffin was angry now. "I have a better wife, a better horse, and a better bard than any of Maelgwn's twenty-four. My bard is also a sorceror and a shape-shifter. No one's better than Taliesin."

Gwyddno put his head in his hands. "Now you've done it," he groaned.

Maelgwn saw one table was not talking. And as soon as he heard that Prince Elffin was boasting he gave a roar of anger. "Fetch him here!"

The guards dragged Elffin up to the King's throne. All talk in the hall died away. The music stopped. Servants stood still with trays of food. Dogs turned their heads.

Everyone stared.

"What's this I hear?" Maelgwn roared. "Are you really saying you can have anything more splendid than me!"

Elffin was scared, but he was still annoyed. He said, "My wife is a better person than yours. For a start she never gets drunk."

Everyone gasped.

The Queen put down her drinking cup.

"My horse is better," Elffin went on. "He never loses a race."

Everyone gasped.

The King turned red with anger.

"And my bard is the best bard in the world," Elffin said. "He could beat this lot easily."

Everyone gasped.

The twenty-four bards all howled.

King Maelgwn stood up. "Well, you've boasted, and now you'll have to prove what you say. I'll test your wife, your horse and your bard. We'll start with your wife. I'll send a messenger to get her drunk."

"He'll never do it. My wife will never get drunk," Elffin said.

Maelgwn laughed. "That's what you think. While we're waiting to find out, we'll go on with the feast. But not you. You can wait in the deepest of my prisons."

The solidiers grabbed Elffin. "You can't do this!" he snapped. "I'm a prince."

"Oh, yes, so you are," Maelgwn sat and poured himself out a drink. "Then I'll make sure your chain is a really splendid one."

They took Elffin down to the darkest dungeon under the castle and tied up his feet and hands with a silver chain.

The moon shone through the window as he sat there on the floor.

I think I may have been a bit unwise about this, he thought.

Chapter 5
The Maid's Finger

Taliesin was lying in the corn-field when he heard the horseman riding along.

He sat up quickly and looked.

The man was wearing rich clothes and his horse was a fine one. He was riding from the north. Taliesin shook his head. He had been expecting trouble and now it was here.

Quickly he turned himself into a red fox and raced home to Elffin's castle before the messenger could arrive. He found Anwen in her hall.

"Listen!" he said.

Anwen stared at the fox. How could a fox talk?

Taliesin turned himself back to a boy. "Sorry. Listen, a messenger is coming from the court. Don't get worried, but I'm afraid Elffin might have been boasting."

"Boasting about what?" she asked.

"You. And me." He paced up and down. "This is what we must do. Find one of the maids and change places with her. Dress her up in your best clothes and load her with necklaces and rings. She must pretend to be you for one night."

Princess Anwen trusted Taliesin. So she asked no more questions. She chose a maid and they swapped clothes. The Princess wore a plain dress and went down and hid in the kitchen.

Taliesin ordered a meal to be made ready.

When the messenger arrived, Taliesin went out to greet him.

Now the messenger was a sly man. His name was Rhun and no one liked him. He was shown up to the Princess's room. The maid stood up, and Taliesin's magic made her look like Anwen, so Rhun was sure this was the Princess.

"Welcome, sir," she said. "Come and dine with me."

Rhun smiled. All evening they ate and drank and at the end of it the maid was so completely drunk she couldn't talk. Rhun

slipped a little powder into her goblet of wine and she fell asleep in her chair. Rhun stood up. "So," he said. "This is the wife who's so much better than Maelgwn's! But I'll need proof to take back to court."

So he cut off the maid's little finger, the one with a fine gold ring on it. Then he slipped out of the castle and rode away.

Taliesin watched him go. "We've been lucky," he said to the Princess. "But now you'd better look after the maid. I must go and rescue Elffin from his troubles."

Rhun galloped fast to the court of Maelgwn and told his story to all the people at the feast. He held up the maid's finger with the ring on it. "And here's the proof," he said.

"Excellent!" Maelgwn was very pleased. He had Elffin brought from the prison and said to him. "Well, your wife isn't so very good, is she? She got so drunk Rhun was able to cut off her finger. So what do you say to that?"

Elffin was shocked, but he didn't show it. He said, "Let me see the finger."

When they showed him the finger, he took one look and gave a great laugh. "What sort of trick is this? First, this finger is so thick my wife's ring hardly fits on it! Second, this finger has long dirty nails! Third, this finger belongs to someone who's been making bread! There's flour under the finger-nails. I can tell you that my wife has thin, clean fingers and she never makes bread. So this proof is false."

Maelgwn was furious. He said, "Well, then we'll test your horse next. It will race against mine tomorrow, and we'll see who wins."

Elffin was dragged back down to the prison.

His father Gwyddno went to inspect Elffin's horse. Elffin had a chestnut horse, and it was very fast, but Maelgwn had a stable full of fast horses.

"How I wish Taliesin was here," Gwyddno muttered.

****

Taliesin arrived at King Maelgwn's castle that morning. There were so many people there for the feast that no one bothered with him.

He watched the King's twenty-four horses being led out onto the race-track. Then he went into the stable and found the boy who was to ride Elffin's horse. "Take these," he said.

He gave the boy twenty-four sticks of holly, burnt black.

"What are they for?" the boy asked.

Taliesin smiled. "As you reach each one of the King's horses in the race, tap it with a holly stick and then throw the stick on the floor."

"What will that do?" the boy asked.

"Wait and see. Oh, and one more thing." Taliesin turned in the door-way. "Sometime during the race, your own horse will stumble and nearly fall. When that happens take off your cap and throw it down to mark the spot."

The boy stared. "Why?"

But Taliesin just smiled.

Chapter 6
Blerm, Blerm

The King and his guests went out to watch the race. King Maelgwn's twenty-four black horses trotted proudly round the field. Then Elffin's one chestnut horse was led out.

Everyone laughed.

Elffin stood in his silver chains between two guards. He felt very scared. If the horse lost he would lose his life. Why had he made such foolish boasts!

Then he saw a thin boy with dark hair standing in the crowd. The boy had a strange, shining face. He winked at Elffin. Was it Taliesin? It must be!

Suddenly Elffin felt a lot better.

The horses lined up. "Go!" Maelgwn roared.

The horses galloped away in a flurry of sand.

At first Elffin's horse was right at the back. But he ran fast, and as he came up to one of Maelgwn's horses, the rider tapped the horse with a holly stick and dropped it to the ground. At once the King's horse slowed down, even though it seemed to be galloping as fast as ever. Elffin's horse went past it.

The crowd groaned.

Maelgwn roared.

Elffin smiled.

The same thing happened with every one of the twenty-four horses. Elffin's rider tapped each of them with a holly stick, and each of them fell behind. Finally Elffin's horse was out in front. No one could catch him now.

As he raced away he stumbled over a tiny hollow in the ground.

At once the rider took off his cap and threw it down. Then he galloped the horse across the finishing line.

Elffin and Gwyddno leapt up and cheered.

All the guests cheered too. They were pleased that for once King Maelgwn's horses hadn't won.

Maelgwn didn't cheer. He turned to Elffin with an angry frown. "All right. Your horse beat all of mine. But there's one part left of your boast, Prince, and this one you'll never win. I have twenty-four of the best bards in Wales. They are so clever no one can out-sing them. Their songs are so difficult that half the time, I don't even understand them myself! So get your one scrawny bard here to my court and we'll hold the last contest of all. And when you lose I'll have your head cut off and I'll stick it on a pole over my gate."

Elffin tried to smile. "My bard will be here today," he said.

They all went back to the court. Elffin had to sit in his chains at the King's table, but Maelgwn and his guests went to their meal. And the feast was more splendid than ever.

Taliesin came into the hall. He made no sound but stood in a corner, near the door that the bards come through. He knew King Maelgwn would summon them at the end of the meal to sing him a song of praise.

Soon a trumpet blew, and the bards arrived.

As they were walking past him, Taliesin puffed his lips out and made a soft "blerm blerm" sound on his lips with one finger.

A baby noise.

A silly noise.

Only one bard saw Taliesin. The others just walked on past.

When they got to the throne the bards stood in a long line and bowed low.

King Maelgwn grinned. "Right, bards! Let's show Prince Elffin what poetry you can sing. Let's show him what real bards should sound like!"

The bards smiled. They were looking forward to this. They tuned up their harps.

They had an excellent new song and they were all going to sing it together.

Maelgwn settled back.

Elffin frowned.

The guests listened.

The bards began their song.

"Blerm blerm," they sang. "Blerm blerm, blerm blerm blerm blerm blerrrrrm. Blerm blerm, blerm blerm ..."

"Stop!" Maelgwn sat up. "What's going on!"

The bards looked at one another in alarm. They started again.

"Blerm blerm, blerm blerm ..."

"STOP!" Maelgwn was on his feet. He was red with rage. "What's wrong with you all! Answer me!"

But they couldn't. All they could say was "Blerm blerm."

"They're drunk!" the King said.

"Well, King," Elffin said softly. "I don't think much of these bards."

Maelgwn was so angry he went along the line hitting each of them. At last one of the bards said something. It was the one who'd seen Taliesin.

"We're not drunk," he spat out. "We've been ... blerm blerm ... enchanted. By a spirit in the form of a ... blerm, blerm ... boy." He turned and pointed. "There he is! There!"

And everyone stared at Taliesin.

Chapter 7
The Song of the Storm

"Did you do this?" Maelgwn asked. "So who are you? Are you human or are you a spirit?"

Taliesin answered –

"I'm Elffin's chief bard.

From the land of summer stars.

I've been flesh and fish

I spent nine months

in Ceridwen's womb.

I've been dead.

I've been alive.

Once I was Gwion.

Now I'm Taliesin."

Maelgwn stared. Never had he heard such a brilliant song before. And yet this was only a boy! He turned to Elffin.

"This is your bard?" he asked.

"That's right, King," Elffin said. "I told you he was amazing. Shall we start the contest now?"

Maelgwn looked all around. There was no way he could get out of it. All the guests – the princes and lords and ladies and bards and bishops – were waiting for him to say something. He had a horrible idea he knew what was going to happen. But he said to his bards, "Sing!"

They tuned their harps. They coughed. And they sang.

"Blerm blerm

blerm blerm

blerrrrm ..."

"Well," Elffin said. "I think we've heard enough of that."

Maelgwn snapped his fingers gloomily and the bards were silent. They glared at Taliesin.

He smiled sweetly back.

"Now it's time for Taliesin to sing," Elffin said. "Pin back your ears, everyone, because I can tell you this will be better than you've ever heard."

Taliesin smiled. He stepped out into the middle of the hall. He called up his magic. And he sang this song –

"Name me this thing.

It lived before the flood.

Not flesh, not bone,

no skin, no blood.

no head, no feet

not young, not old.

It crushes the woods,

flattens the fold,

crashes on coasts

stamps on farms

wrecks whole forests,

strokes the corn.

It's wide as the earth

narrow as breath

invisible yet seen.

Instant confusion!

It's free, it's wild

It's meek, it's mild,

silent as a shiver,

the loudest thing ever.

Fear and fun,

now here, now there

hot as the sun

cold as winter.

Here it comes to make war

On Maelgwn's anger!"

While he was singing they began to hear a terrible sound outside, rising and howling. Everyone looked around.

"The wind," Elffin shouted. "The answer is the wind."

Taliesin smiled. He lifted his arms high and a great howling storm came out of the night. It roared over the roof and slammed all the doors wide open. It swept inside and hurled all the cups and plates into the air. Bards were blown sideways. Ladies' cloaks flapped in their faces. Maelgwn was thrown back into his chair.

They were all terrified that the castle would collapse about them.

"Stop!" Maelgwn yelled. "Stop now!"

Chapter 8
Elffin's Reward

"Please!" Maelgwn howled. "Stop the wind."

Taliesin shook his head. "Not until the Prince is free."

The whole building shuddered. The storm burst all the windows open.

Maelgwn yelled, "Do as he says!"

The guards fought their way across to Elffin and unlocked the silver chain. It fell around his feet and he stepped out of it.

As soon as Taliesin saw Elffin was free he changed his song, and the wind stopped. The people stood up and brushed off their clothes and stared around. The splendid hall was looking a bit of a mess now.

Taliesin sang, "I was born from the cauldron

of magic and spells.

Be still, bards

and listen to me.

You are like crows

cawing your song.

No one will ever

sing like Taliesin."

"Well that's true," Maelgwn said. He turned to Elffin. "Forgive me, Prince Elffin. You have proved your boasts were true. First, your wife."

"And here I am." Anwen pushed through the crowd. She smiled at Elffin and held up her hand, so that everyone could see all her fingers were still there. "I've never been drunk, as you can see, and I've come for my ring back."

Maelgwn gave her the ring.

Then he said, "And then your horse beat all my twenty-four. As for your bard, well, he is indeed the best in the world. You're safe, Prince Elffin. You can go home now. I'll take care not to invite you here again."

All the people clapped and cheered.

Taliesin took his spell off the bards, so that they could talk and sing again. They all agreed he was the best bard among them. But they weren't very happy about it. Elffin and Anwen and Taliesin and Gwyddno and all their men set off for home. As they rode away, along the sea shore, they came to the place where the race had been, and there was the rider's cap lying on the sand.

Elffin looked at his rider. "Why is that there?"

The boy said, "Taliesin told me to throw it down where the horse stumbled."

Taliesin smiled. "So I did. Order your men to dig there, Prince Elffin, and see what they find."

So two of the men got down from their horses and dug into the hollow. And when they had dug deep enough they found a great bronze cauldron full of gold coins.

Anwen said, "Look at that!"

Gwyddno said, "That's what I call luck!"

Elffin just stared.

Taliesin said, "There you are, Prince. That's your reward for taking me out of the weir in my leather bag, and looking after me all these years. I told you I'd be more use to you than fish."

So they took the gold away with them and a pool of water rose up where the pot had been and filled the hole, which is still called Cauldron Pool. From that time on, all over Wales, Taliesin was known as the greatest bard and sorceror and shape-shifter in the world.

And however much Elffin boasted about it, nobody ever dared argue with him again.

How to Say the Characters' Names

Ceridwen   Ker *id* wen

Morfran   *More* vran

Gwion   *Gwi* on

Taliesin   Tal *yes* in

King Gwyddno   King *Gwith* no

Elffin   *El* fin

Anwen   *An* wen

King Maelgwn   King *Mile* gon

Rhun   Rinn

Catherine Fisher

Author

Favourite hero:
Merlin, one of the great Welsh heroes. He was a hero not because he was good at fighting, but because he was good at thinking and working things out.

Favourite monster:
Grendel, the monster in the poem *Beowulf*. A terrible beast who lives in the swamp.

Your weapon of choice:
A sword. I've always loved fencing (fighting with blunt swords). In fact, I've been a fencer since I was 12, so I'm pretty good with swords!

RELOADED

Peter Clover

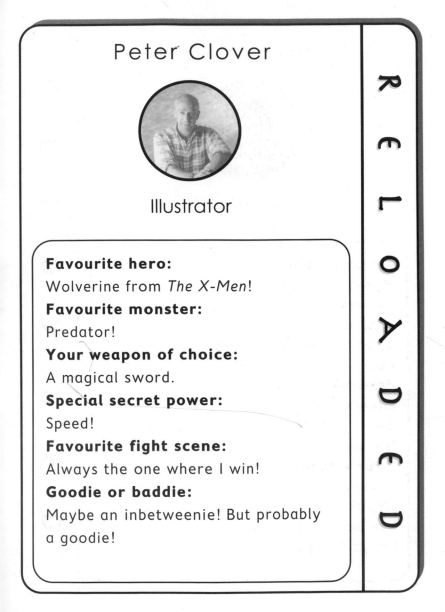

Illustrator

Favourite hero:
Wolverine from *The X-Men*!

Favourite monster:
Predator!

Your weapon of choice:
A magical sword.

Special secret power:
Speed!

Favourite fight scene:
Always the one where I win!

Goodie or baddie:
Maybe an inbetweenie! But probably
a goodie!

RELOADED

Barrington Stoke would like to thank all its readers for commenting on the manuscript before publication and in particular:

Helen Cox
James Cox
Matthew Donkin
Susan Donkin
Libby Fazakerley
Cameron French
Freddy Goodall
David Griswold
Megan Heywood
Jake Morgan
Helen O'Connell
Jennifer O'Connell
Anna Stokes

Become a Consultant!

Would you like to be a consultant? Ask your parent, carer or teacher to contact us at the email address below – we'd love to hear from them! They can also find out more by visiting our website.

schools@barringtonstoke.co.uk
www.barringtonstoke.co.uk